If I Wrote
a Book About You

For Luke and Sylvie -SA

For my daughter, Hazel Lou -DH

Published in 2014 by Simply Read Books www.simplyreadbooks.com

Text © 2014 Stephany Aulenback Illustrations © 2014 Denise Holmes

Library and Archives Canada Cataloguing in Publication

Aulenback, Stephany, author
If I wrote a book about you / written by Stephany Aulenback
and illustrated by Denise Holmes.

ISBN 978-1-927018-46-0

I. Holmes, Denise, illustrator II. Title.

PS8601.U4413 2014   jC813'.6   C2013-906053-7

We gratefully acknowledge for their financial support of our publishing program the Canada Council for the Arts, the BC Arts Council, and the Government of Canada through the Canada Book Fund (CBF).

Manufactured in Malaysia

Book design by Sara Gillingham Studio

10 9 8 7 6 5 4 3 2 1

If I Wrote
a Book About You

by Stephany Aulenback • illustrated by Denise Holmes

SIMPLY READ BOOKS

If I wrote a book about you
and how wonderful you are,
I would write it everywhere.

captivating

I would write that you are captivating
with the branches of the trees.

I would write that you are perfect in the sand on the beach.

I would write that
you are entertaining
with the toys on the floor.

I would write that
you are clever with the
crumbs from your crackers.

With the flowers on the front lawn,
I would spell out that you are magnificent,

and with the vegetables growing in the
garden, I would say that you are strong.

With the peas on your plate, I would write that you are delectable,

and that
you are
delicious
with the
noodles in
your soup.

I would write that you are amazing with the telephone wires, amazing

and that you are fascinating with the yellow lines

that run down the middle of the road.

.49¢

$2.99

.50¢

Green's
Grocery

OPEN

fascinating

With the beads on a bracelet, I would write that you are charming.

With the bubbles in your bathwater, I would spell out that you are adorable.

mesmerizing

I would write that you are mesmerizing with the raindrops on the window panes,

and that you are precious
with the pennies on the pavement.

On the fortunes
inside fortune cookies,
I would write that
you are remarkable,

and with the candies decorating your
birthday cake, I would write that you are sweet.

With the rays
from the sun,
I would write
that you are
radiant.

With the beams from the moon, I would write that you are shining.

And with the
stars in the sky,
I would write that
you are beautiful.

I would write that you are lovable
in the freckles on your face.

And in the wrinkles on mine,
I would write that you are loved.

If I wrote a book about you,
I would write it everywhere,
and it would tell all the world,
and all the world would tell . . .

YOUR BOOK

by MOM

. . . how wonderful you are.